Captain Corelli's Mandolin
Louis de Bernières

WH S LITTLE READS

This extract first published in the UK in 2003 exclusively for
WHSmith Limited, Greenbridge Road, Swindon SN3 3LD
www.WHSmith.co.uk

Random House, 20 Vauxhall Bridge Road, London, SW1V 2SA

To celebrate the BBC's The Big Read

Cover design template copyright © 2003 WHSmith Limited

Copyright © Louis de Bernières, 1994

Captain Corelli's Mandolin was first published in
the United Kingdom in 1994 by Secker & Warburg
Published by Vinatge in 1998

ISBN 0 0994 6676 7

Typeset by Palimpsest Book Production Limited,
Polmont, Stirlingshire

Printed in Great Britain by Cox & Wyman, Reading

Captain Corelli's Mandolin

Resistance

All over the island there was a burgeoning of graf-
fiti that took merry or malicious advantage of the
fact that the Italians could not decipher the Cyrillic
script. They mistook Rs for Ps, did not know that
Gs can look like Ys or inverted Ls, had no idea
what the triangle was, thought that an E was an
H, construed theta as a kind of O, did not appreciate that the letter in the shape of a tent was the
same as the one that looked like an inverted Y,
were baffled by the three horizontal strokes that
could also be written as a squiggle, knew from
mathematics that pi meant 22 divided by 7, were
unaware that E the wrong way round was an S,
that the Y could also be written as a V and was in
fact an E, were confused by the existence of an O
with a vertical stroke that was actually an F, did
not understand that the X was a K, failed utterly

to find anything that might be meant by the elegant trident, and found that the omega reminded them of an earring. Ergo, conditions were ideal for the nocturnal splashing of white paint in huge letters on all available walls, especially as the quirks of an individual's handwriting could render the letters even more completely inscrutable. ENOSIS fought for space with ELEPHTHERIA, 'Long Live The King' cohabited without apparent anomaly with 'Workers Of The World Unite', 'Wops fuck off' abutted with 'Duce, Eat My Shit'. An admirer of Lord Byron wrote, 'I dream'd that Greece might still be free' in wobbly Roman letters, and General Tsolakoglou, the new quisling leader of the Greek people, appeared everywhere as a cartoon figure, committing various obscene and unpleasant acts with the Duce.

In the kapheneia and fields the men related Italian jokes: How many gears does an Italian tank have? One forward and four in reverse. What is the shortest book in the world? *The Italian Book of War Heroes.* How many Italians does it take to put in a light-bulb? One to hold the bulb and two hundred to rotate the room. What is the name of

Hitler's dog? Benito Mussolini. Why do Italians wear moustaches? To be reminded of their mothers. In the encampments the Italian soldiers in their turn asked, 'How do you know when a Greek girl is having a period?' And the answer would be 'She is wearing only one sock.' It was a long interlude during which the two populations stood off from each other, defusing by means of jokes the guilty suspicion on the one side and the livid resentment on the other. The Greeks talked fierily in secret about the partisans, about forming a resistance, and the Italians confined themselves to camp, the only signs of activity being the setting up of batteries, a daily reconnaissance by amphibious aircraft, and a mounted curfew patrol that jogged about at dusk, its members more anxious to exercise charm on females than to enforce an early night. Then a decision was made to billet officers upon suitable members of the local population.

The first thing about it that Pelagia knew was when she returned from the well, only to find a rotund Italian officer, accompanied by a sergeant and a private, standing in the kitchen, looking around with an appraising expression, and making notes with a pencil so blunt that he was obliged to read what he had written by casting the indentations against the light.

Pelagia had already stopped fearing that she was going to be raped, and had become accustomed to scowling at leers and slapping at the hands that made exploratory pinches of the backside; the Italians had turned out to be the modest kind of Romeo that is resigned to being rebuffed, but does not abandon hope. Nonetheless, she felt a momentary leap of fear when she came in and found the soldiers, and, but for a moment of indecision, she would have turned tail and fled. The plump officer smiled expansively, raised his arms in a gesture that signified, 'I would explain if I could, but I don't speak Greek,' and said, 'Ah,' in a manner that signified, 'How delightful to see you, since you are so pretty, and I am embarrassed to be in your kitchen, but what else can I do?' Pelagia said, 'Aspettami, vengo,' and ran to fetch her father from the kapheneion.

The soldiers waited, as requested, and soon Pelagia reappeared with her father, who was anticipating the encounter with some trepidation. There was a lurch of dread waiting to surge into his heart and weaken it, but also a cold and detached courage that comes to those who are determined to resist oppression with dignity; he remembered his advice to the boys in the kapheneion – 'Let us use our anger wisely' – and squared his shoulders. He wished that he had retained his moustache with the waxed tips, so that he might twist its extremities balefully and censoriously.

'Buon giorno,' said the officer, holding out his hand hopefully. The doctor perceived the conciliatory nature of the gesture and its lack of conqueror's hubris, and much to his own surprise he reached out and shook the proffered hand.

'Buon giorno,' he replied. 'I do hope that you enjoy your regrettably short stay on our island.'

The officer raised his eyebrows, 'Short?'

'You have been expelled from Libya and Ethiopia,' the doctor said, leaving the Italian to extrapolate his meaning.

'You speak Italian very well,' said the officer, 'you are the first one I have come across. We are very badly in need of translators to work with the populace. There would be privileges. It seems that no one here speaks Italian.'

'I think you mean that none of you speak Greek.'

'Just so, as you say. It was only an idea.'

'You are very kind,' said Dr Iannis acidly, 'but I think you will find that those of us who do speak Italian will suddenly lose our memory when required to do so.'

The officer laughed, 'Understandable under the circumstances. I meant no offence.'

'There is Pasquale Lacerba, the photographer. He is an Italian who lives in Argostoli, but perhaps even he would not like to co-operate. But he is young enough not to know better. As for me, I am a doctor, and I have enough to do without becoming a collaborator.'

'It's worth a try,' said the quartermaster, 'most of the time we don't understand anything.'

'It's just as well,' observed the doctor. 'Perhaps you could tell me why you're here?'

'Ah,' said the man, shifting uneasily, aware of the unpleasantness of his position, 'the fact is, I am sorry to say, and with great regret, that . . . we shall be obliged to billet an officer on these premises.'

'There are only two rooms, my daughter's and my own. This is quite impossible, and it is also, as you probably realise, an outrage. I must refuse.' The doctor bristled like an angry cat, and the officer scratched his head with his pencil. It was really very awkward that the doctor spoke Italian; in other houses he had avoided this kind of scene and left it to the unfortunate guests to explain the situation, by means of grunts and gesticulations, when they turned up unannounced with their kitbags and drivers. The two men looked at one another, the doctor tilting his chin at a proud angle, and the Italian searching for a form of words that was both firm and mollifying. Suddenly the doctor's expression changed, and he asked, 'Did you say that you are a quartermaster?'

'No, Signor Dottore, you seem to have worked it out for yourself. I am a quartermaster. Why?'

'So do you have access to medical supplies?'

'Naturally,' replied the officer, 'I have access to everything.' The two men exchanged glances, divining perfectly the train of the other's thought.

Dr Iannis said, 'I am short of many things, and the war has made it worse.'

'And I am short of accommodation. So?'

'So it's a deal,' said the doctor.

'A deal,' repeated the quartermaster. 'Anything you want, you send me a message via Captain Corelli. I am sure you will find him very charming. By the way, do you know anything about corns? Our doctors are useless.'

'For your corns I would probably need morphia, hypodermic syringes, sulphur ointment and iodine, neosalvarsan, bandages and lint, surgical spirit, salicylic acid, scalpels, and collodion,' said the doctor, 'but I will need a great deal, if you understand me. In the meantime get a pair of boots that fits you.'

When the quartermaster had gone, taking with him the details of the doctor's requirements, Pelagia took her father's elbow anxiously and asked, 'But Papas, where is he to sleep? Am I to cook for him? And what with? There is almost no food.'

'He will have my bed,' said the doctor, knowing perfectly well that Pelagia would protest.

'O no, Papas, he will have mine. I will sleep in the kitchen.'

'Since you insist, koritsimou. Just think of all the medicine and equipment it will mean for us.' He rubbed his hands together and added, 'The secret of being occupied is to exploit the exploiters. It is also knowing how to resist. I think we shall be very horrible to this captain.'

In the early evening Captain Corelli arrived, driven by his new baritone, Bombardier Carlo Piero Guercio. The jeep skidded to a halt outside, generating clouds of dust and much noisy alarm amongst the chickens that were scratching in the road, and the two men came in by the entrance of the yard. Carlo looked at the olive tree, amazed by its size, and the captain looked around, appreciating the signs of a quiet domestic life. There was a goat tied to the tree, washing hanging on a line from the tree to the house, a vivid bougainvillaea and a trailing vine, an old table upon which there lay a small heap of chopped onions. There was also a young woman with dark eyes, a scarf tied around her head, and in her hand was a large cooking knife. The captain fell to his knees before her and exclaimed dramatically, 'Please don't kill me, I am innocent.'

'Don't worry about him,' said Carlo, 'he is always being foolish. He can't help it.'

Pelagia smiled, against her will and against her resolutions, and caught Carlo's eye. He was huge, as big as Velisarios. Two ordinary men might have fitted inside one leg of his breeches, and she could have made two shirts for her father from the one that he wore. The captain sprang to his feet. 'I am Captain Antonio Corelli, but you may call me maestro if you wish, and this . . .' he took Carlo by the arm '. . . is one of our heroes. He has a hundred medals for saving life, and none for taking it.'

'It's nothing,' said Carlo, smiling diffidently. Pelagia looked up at the towering soldier, and knew intuitively that, despite his size, despite his enormous hands that might fit about the neck of an ox, he was a soft and saddened man. 'A brave Italian is a freak of nature,' she said sourly, remembering her father's instructions to be as unaccommodating as possible.

Corelli protested. 'He rescued a fallen comrade

in the open field, under fire. He is famous all over the Army, and he refused promotion too. He is a one-man ambulance. What a man he is. He has a Greek bullet in his leg to show for it. And this . . .' he tapped a case in his hand '. . . is Antonia. Perhaps we will make more formal introductions later on. She is very anxious to meet you, as am I. By what name do men know you, may I ask?'

Pelagia looked at him properly for the first time, and realised with a start that this was the very same officer who had commanded his platoon of comedians to march past at the eyes left. She blushed. At the same moment Corelli recognised her, and he bit his lower lip in mockery of himself. 'Ah,' he exclaimed, and slapped himself on the wrist. He fell to his knees once more, hung his head in sly penitence, and said softly, 'Forgive me, Father, for I have sinned. Mea culpa, mea culpa, mea maxima culpa.' He beat his breast and wiped away an imaginary tear.

Carlo exchanged glances with Pelagia, and shrugged his shoulders. 'He's always like this.'

Dr Iannis came out, saw the captain on his knees before his daughter, caught her bemused expression, and said, 'Captain Corelli? I want a word with you. Now.'

Startled by the authority in the older man's voice, Corelli stood up, abashed, and held out his hand. The doctor withheld his own, and said crisply, 'I want an explanation.'

'Of what? I have done nothing. You must excuse me, I was only joking with your daughter.' He shifted nervously, unhappily conscious of the possibility that he had made a bad start.

'I want to know why you have defaced the monument.'

'The monument? Forgive me, but . . .'

'The monument, the one in the middle of the bridge that de Bosset built. It has been defaced.'

The captain knitted his brows in perplexity, and then his face lightened, 'Ah, you mean the one across the bay at Argostoli. Why, what has happened to it?'

'It had "To The Glory Of The British People" inscribed on the obelisk. I have heard that some of your soldiers have chipped away the letters. Do you think you can so easily erase our history? Are you so stupid that you think that we will forget

16

what it said? Is this how you wage war, by the chipping away of letters? What kind of heroism is this?' The doctor raised his voice to a new note of vehemence, 'Tell me how you would like it if we defaced the tombstones in the Italian cemetery, captain.'

'I had nothing to do with it, Signor. You are blaming the wrong man. I apologise for the offence, but . . .' he shrugged his shoulders '. . . the decision was not mine, and neither were the soldiers.'

The doctor scowled and raised his finger, stabbing the air, 'There would be no tyranny, captain, and no wars, if minions did not ignore their conscience.'

The captain looked to Pelagia, as though in expectation of support, and suffered the unbearable sensation of having been sent back to school. 'I must protest,' he said feebly.

'You cannot protest, because there is no excuse. And why, will you tell me, has the teaching of Greek history been prohibited in our schools? Why is everyone being obliged to learn Italian, eh?'

Pelagia smiled to herself; she could not have calculated how often she had heard her father divagating upon the absolute necessity and perfect reasonableness of having compulsory Italian in schools.

The captain felt himself wanting to squirm like a little boy who has been caught stealing sweets from the tin reserved for Sundays. 'In the Italian Empire,' he said, the words tasting bitter on his tongue, 'it is logical that everyone should learn Italian . . . I believe that that is the reason. I am not responsible for it, I repeat.' He began visibly to perspire. The doctor shot him a glance that was intended to be, and was, deeply withering. 'Pathetic,' he said, and turned on his heel. He went indoors and sat down at his desk, very satisfied with himself. He leaned forward, annoyed Psipsina by tickling her whiskers, and confided to her, 'Got him on the run already.'

Outside in the yard Captain Corelli was dumbfounded, and Pelagia was feeling sorry for him. 'Your father is . . .' he said, and the words failed him. 'Yes, he is,' confirmed Pelagia.

'Where am I to sleep?' asked Corelli, glad of anything that might be a distraction, all his good humour having dried to dust.

'You will have my bed,' said Pelagia.

Under normal circumstances Antonio Corelli would have asked brightly, 'Are we to share it then? How hospitable,' but now, after the doctor's words, he was appalled by this information. 'It's out of the question,' he said briskly. 'Tonight I shall sleep in the yard, and tomorrow I shall request alternative accommodation.'

Pelagia was shocked by the feelings of alarm that arose in her breast. Could it be that there was something inside her that wanted this foreigner, this interloper, to stay? She went inside and relayed the Italian's decision to her father. 'He can't go,' he said. 'How am I supposed to browbeat him if he isn't here? And anyway, he seems like a personable boy.'

'Papakis, you made him feel like a flea. I almost felt sorry for him.'

'You did feel sorry for him, koritsimou. I saw it in your face.' He took his daughter's arm and went back out with her. 'Young man,' he said to the captain, 'you are staying here, whether you like it or not. It is quite possible that your quartermaster will decide to impose someone even worse.'

'But your daughter's bed, Dottore? It would not be ... it would be a terrible thing.'

'She will be comfortable in the kitchen, captain. I don't care how bad you feel, that is not my problem. I am not the aggressor. Do you understand me?'

'Yes,' said the captain, overpowered, and not entirely grasping what was happening to him.

'Kyria Pelagia will bring water, some coffee, and some mezedakia to eat. You will find that we do not lack hospitality. It is our tradition, captain, to be hospitable even to those who do not merit it. It is a question of honour, a motive which you may find somewhat foreign and unfamiliar. Your sizeable friend is welcome to join us.'

Carlo and the captain uneasily partook of the tiny spinach pies, the fried baby squid and the dolmades stuffed with rice. The doctor glowered at them, inwardly delighted with the successful inauguration of his novel project for resistance, and the two soldiers avoided his gaze, commenting politely and inconsequentially upon the beauty of the night, the impossible size of the olive tree, and any and every irrelevance that occurred to them.

Carlo drove gratefully away, and the captain sat on Pelagia's bed miserably. It was the time for an evening meal, and despite the plates of appetisers his stomach growled from force of habit. The thought of more of that wonderful food left him feeling weak. The doctor came in once and told him, 'The answer to your problem is to eat a lot of onions, tomatoes, parsley, basil, oregano, and garlic. The garlic will be an antiseptic for the fissures, and the other things, taken together, will soften the stools. It is very important not to strain at all, and if you eat meat, it must always be accompanied by a great deal of fluid and a sideplate of vegetables.'

The captain watched him leave the room, and felt more humiliated than he had ever thought possible. How could the old man possibly have known that he suffered from haemorrhoids?

In the kitchen the doctor asked Pelagia whether or not she had noticed that the captain walked very carefully and occasionally winced.

Father and daughter sat down to eat, both of them clattering the cutlery on the plates, and waited until they were sure that the Italian must

21

be dying of hunger and feeling like a ragamuffin boy who has been sent to Coventry at school, and then they invited him to join them. He sat with them and ate in silence.

'This is Cephallonian meat pie,' said the doctor in an informative tone of voice, 'except that, thanks to your people, it doesn't have any meat in it.'

Afterwards, when the curfew patrol had already passed, the doctor announced his intention to go for a walk. 'But the curfew . . .' protested Corelli, and the doctor replied, 'I was born here, this is my island.' He gathered up his hat and his pipe, and swept out.

'I must insist,' he called vainly after the doctor, who prudently circled about the house and waited a quarter of an hour as he sat upon the wall, eavesdropping on the conversation of the two young people.

Pelagia looked at Corelli as he sat at the table, and felt the need to comfort him. 'What is Antonia?' she asked.

He avoided her eyes, 'My mandolin. I am a musician.'

'A musician? In the Army?'

'When I joined, Kyria Pelagia, Army life consisted mainly of being paid for sitting about doing nothing. Plenty of time for practice, you see. I had a plan to become the best mandolin player in Italy, and then I would leave the Army and earn a living. I didn't want to be a café player, I wanted to play Hummel and Conforto and Giuliani. There's not much demand, so you have to be very good.'

'You mean you're a soldier by mistake?' asked Pelagia, who had never heard of any of these composers.

'It was a plan that went wrong; the Duce got some big ideas.' He looked at her wistfully.

'After the war,' she said.

He nodded and smiled, 'After the war.'

'I want to be a doctor,' said Pelagia, who had not even mentioned this idea to her father.

That night, just as she was drifting off to sleep beneath her blankets, she heard a muffled cry, and shortly afterwards the captain appeared in the kitchen, a little wide-eyed, a towel wrapped about his waist. She sat up, clutching the blankets about her breasts.

'Forgive me,' he said, perceiving her alarm, 'but there appears to be an enormous weasel on my bed.'

Pelagia laughed, 'That's not a weasel, that's Psipsina. She is our pet. She always sleeps on my bed.'

'What is it?'

Pelagia could not resist essaying her father's mode of resistance: 'Haven't you heard of Greek cats?'

The captain looked at her suspiciously, shrugged his shoulders, and returned to his room. He approached the pine marten and stroked it on the forehead with a tentative forefinger. It felt very soft and comforting. 'Micino, micino,' he cooed speculatively, and fondled her ears. Psipsina sniffed at the wiggling digit, did not recognise it, surmised that it might be edible, and bit it.

Captain Antonio Corelli snatched his hand away, watched the beads of blood well out of his finger, and fought against the shamingly childish tears that were rising unbidden to his eyes. He attempted by force of will to suppress the mounting sting of the bite, and knew for certain that he had been pierced through to the bone. Never, in all his

24

life, had he felt so unloved. These Greeks. When they said 'ne' it meant 'yes', when they nodded it meant 'no', and the more angry they were, the more they smiled. Even the cats were from another planet, and moreover could have no possible motive for such malice.

He lay abjectly upon the hard cold floor, unable to sleep, until at last Psipsina missed Pelagia, and went off to look for her. He climbed back into the bed and sank gratefully into the mattress. 'Mmm,' he said to himself, and realised that he was savouring a lingering, vanishing smell of young woman. He thought about Pelagia for a while, remembering the clean scoop of white flesh as the neck became the breast and shoulder, and finally fell asleep.

He woke in the night, suffering from the sensation that his neck was abominably hot and that his chin was ticklish. As he emerged into awareness it became horribly evident that the Greek cat had wrapped itself about his neck and was fast asleep. Horrified and afraid, he tried to move a little. The animal growled sleepily.

He lay paralysed for what seemed like hours,

sweating, resisting the itching and the unnatural warmth, listening to the owls and the unholy noises of the night. At some point he noticed that the encumbrance across his neck smelled consolingly sweet. It was an aroma that mingled pleasantly with the smell of Pelagia. He drifted away at last, and for some reason dreamed irrelevantly of elephants, bakelite, and horses.

Sharp Edges

The hour shortly after dawn found Captain Antonio Corelli waiting in vain at the entrance to the yard for Carlo to come and fetch him away. The latter had broken a shackle on the suspension of his jeep, and was engaged in kicking the tyres and swearing at the profound potholes in the road that had undone his early start. He already possessed a deep horror of letting down the captain, a horror shared by all the men who served under him, and his fractious ill-temper was exacerbated when he tried to light a cigarette, only to find that the desiccated rod of powdery tobacco slid out of its tube of paper and smouldered insolently in the dust, leaving him with a piece of scorchingly hot paper that stuck tenaciously to his lower lip. He pulled the paper away, and it removed a tag of skin. He licked the stinging wound, touched it with his finger, and cursed the Germans for their success in monopolising the supplies of the best tobacco. A thin old peasant mounted sidesaddle on a donkey passed him by, saw the broken state of the vehicle as it sagged to one side, smiled with satisfaction, and raised a hand in a gesture of casual greeting. Carlo gritted his teeth and smiled. 'Fuck the war,' he said, since one greeting was as good as another to a Greek. It looked as though there would be no La Scala that morning, unless the opera society could manage the Soldiers' Chorus on its own. He abandoned the jeep and began to trudge towards the village.

Velisarios passed him, and the two men looked at one another with something like recognition. However thin and bedraggled he had become since he had gone to the front, Velisarios was still the biggest man that anyone had ever seen, and Carlo, despite his equivalent experiences on the other side of the line, was also the biggest man that anyone had ever seen. Both of these Titans had become accustomed to the saddening suspicion within themselves that they were freaks; to be superhuman was a burden that had seemed impossible to share and impossible to explain to ordinary people, who would have been incredulous.

They were both astonished, and for a moment forgot that they were enemies. 'Hey,' exclaimed Velisarios, raising his hands in a gesture of pleasure. Carlo, stumped for an exclamation that would make sense to a Greek, aimed inaccurately for a failed compromise that sounded very like 'Ung'. Carlo offered one of his atrocious cigarettes, Velisarios took one, and they gesticulated and made sour faces to each other as they drew on the smoke that was sharp as needles. 'Fuck the war,' said Carlo, by way of farewell, and the two went on their opposite ways, Carlo beginning to feel very content. A kilometre away, Velisarios came across the crippled jeep, paused in thought, and went to fetch a friend. He returned, lifted the vehicle at each corner in turn, and his companion removed the wheels. Then he drained the water from the radiator, and refilled it with petrol from the jerrycan strapped to the back.

Corelli continued to wait. The doctor passed by on his way to the kapheneion, in an anticipatory state of annoyance on account of the fact that the coffee being served these days tasted of river mud and tar, and was becoming more expensive by the second. 'Buon giorno,' called the captain, and the doctor turned. 'I trust that you slept badly,' he said.

The captain smiled resignedly, 'For some reason I dreamed about animals made of bakelite. They were like dolphins with sharp edges, and they were leaping about. It was very disturbing. Also, your cat bit me.' He held out the wounded finger, and the doctor inspected it. 'It's very swollen,' he said, 'and it will probably go septic. Pine martens can have a nasty bite. If I were you I would show it to a doctor.' With that he went on his way, leaving the captain to repeat foolishly, 'Pine martens?' He realised that Pelagia had only made a small joke at his expense, but, curiously, it left him feeling let down and very gullible.

When Pelagia came out she found the usurper of her bed throwing Lemoni up and down in the air by the armpits. The child was whooping and laughing, and it appeared that what was transpiring was a lesson in Italian. 'Bella fanciulla,' the captain was saying. He was waiting for Lemoni to repeat it. 'Bla fanshla,' she giggled, and the captain threw her up, exclaiming, 'No, no, bella fanciulla.' He dwelt lovingly upon the doubled L, waited for Lemoni to descend, and raised an eyebrow as he awaited her next attempt. 'Bla flanshla,' she said triumphantly, only to be launched skyward again.

Pelagia smiled as she watched, and then Lemoni saw her. The captain followed the cast of her glance, and straightened up, a little embarrassed, 'Buon giorno, Kyria Pelagia. It seems that my driver has been delayed.'

'What's it mean, what's it mean?' demanded Lemoni, whose faith in the omniscience of adults was such that she was sure that Pelagia would be able to tell her. Pelagia patted her cheek, cleared the strands of hair from her eyes, and told her, 'It means "pretty puss", koritsimou. Off you go now, I'm sure that someone is missing you.'

The little girl skipped away in her usual capricious and erratic manner, waving her arms and chanting, 'Bla, bla, bla. Bla, bla, bla.'

Corelli reproached Pelagia, 'Why did you send her away? We were having a wonderful time.'

'Fraternisation,' answered Pelagia. 'It's indecent, even in a child.'

Corelli's face fell, and he scuffed the toe of his boot in the dust. He looked up the sky, dropped his head, and sighed. Without looking at Pelagia, he said with heartfelt sincerity, 'Signorina, in times like this, in a war, all of us have to make the most of what little innocent pleasure there is.'

Pelagia saw the resignation and weariness in his face, and felt ashamed of herself. In the silence that followed, both of them reflected upon their own unworthiness. Then the captain said, 'One day I would like a pretty puss like that, for my own,' and without awaiting a reply he set off in the direction from which he expected Carlo to come.

Pelagia watched him leave, thinking her own thoughts. His retreating back had about it a poignant air of solitude. Then she went inside, took down the two volumes of *The Complete and Concise Home Doctor*, opened them out on the table, and guiltlessly read the sections about reproduction, venereal infections, parturition, and the scrotum. She proceeded at random to read about cascarilla, furred tongue, the anus and its disorders, and anxiety.

Fearing the return of her father from the

kapheneion, she finally replaced the books on
their shelf, and began to think of reasons for
delaying her necessary trip to the well. She
chopped some onions, unclear as to what recipe
she was intending them to be a part of, but
anxious that her father should be able to perceive
some concrete evidence of activity, and then she
went outside to brush her oblivious goat. She
found two ticks and a small swelling in the loose
skin of the haunch. She worried about whether
or not she should be worried about this, and then
began to think about the captain. Mandras caught
her dreaming.

He had climbed out of bed, cursing and
completely cured, on the day of the invasion. It
was as if the advent of the Italians had been something so important, so weighty, that it precluded
the luxury of indulging in his illness. The doctor
had affected to be unsurprised, but Drosoula and
Pelagia had agreed that there was something
suspicious about an affliction that could be
switched off with such a virtuoso flourish.
Mandras had gone down to the sea and swum
with his dolphins as though he had never been

away, and had returned refreshed, the salt water drying in his tousled hair, a smile upon his face, the muscles in his torso uncontracted, and had climbed the hill with a mullet to present to Pelagia. He had ruffled Psipsina's ears, swung briefly in the olive tree, and had left the impression on Pelagia of being madder in his new sanity than he had been when he was mad. She felt guilty now, whenever she saw him, and deeply uncomfortable.

She started when he tapped her on the shoulder, and despite the effort to force a radiant smile he did not fail to see the flicker of alarm in her eyes. He ignored it, but would remember it later. 'Hello,' he said, 'is your father in? I've still got some bad skin on my arm.'

Glad of something objective upon which to focus her attention, she said, 'Let me look at it,' whereupon he said brightly, 'I was hoping to see the organ-grinder rather than the monkey.'

Mandras had heard this metaphor at the front, had liked it, and had waited a long time for an opportunity to use it. It had struck him as witty, and he had thought that what was witty was also likely to be charming. He wanted nothing so much as to be able to charm Pelagia back into the affection that he unhappily feared that he had lost.

But Pelagia's eyes flashed fire, and Mandras' heart sank. 'I didn't mean it,' he said, 'it was a joke.' The two young people looked at one another, as though sharing an appreciation of all that was gone, and then Mandras said, 'I'm going to join the partisans.'

'Oh,' she said.

He shrugged, 'I haven't any choice. I'm leaving tomorrow. I'll take my boat to Manolas.'

Pelagia was horrified, 'What about the submarines? And the warships? It's madness.'

'It's worth the risk if I go at night. I can sail by the stars. I was thinking of tomorrow night.'

There was a long silence. Pelagia said, 'I won't be able to write.'

'I know.'

Pelagia went inside a moment and came out bearing the waistcoat that she had so devotedly made and embroidered whilst her fiancé had been at the front. She showed it to him diffidently, saying, 'This is what I was making for you, to dance at feasts. Do you want to take it now?'

Mandras took it and held it up. He cocked his head to one side and said, 'It doesn't quite match up, does it? I mean, the pattern is a little different on each side.'

Pelagia felt a pang of disappointment that tasted of betrayal. 'I tried so hard,' she exclaimed piteously, in a rush of emotion, 'and I can never please you.'

Mandras smote his forehead with the heel of his palm, screwed up his face in self-criticism, and said, 'O God, I am sorry. I didn't mean it the way it came out.' He sighed and shook his head. 'Ever since I went away, my mouth and my heart and my brain don't seem so well connected. Everything is upside down.'

Pelagia took back the waistcoat and told him, 'I'll try to put it right. What does your mother say?'

He looked at her appealingly, 'I was hoping that you could tell her. I couldn't bear to hear her weeping and pleading if I tell her myself.'

Pelagia laughed bitterly, 'Are you such a coward, then?'

'I am with my mother,' he confessed. 'Please tell her.'

'All right. All right, I will. She has lost a husband and now she loses a son.'

'I'll be back,' he said.

She shook her head slowly, and sighed, 'Promise me one thing.' He nodded, and she continued, 'Whenever you are about to do something terrible, think of me, and then don't do it.'

'I'm a Greek,' he said gently, 'not a Fascist. And I will think of you every minute.'

She heard the touching sincerity in his voice, and felt herself wanting to cry. Spontaneously they embraced, as though they were brother and sister rather than two betrothed, and then they gazed for a moment into each other's eyes. 'God go with you,' said Pelagia, and he smiled sadly, 'And with you.'

'I shall always remember you swinging in the tree.'

'And me falling on the pot.'

They laughed together a moment, and then he looked at her longingly for one last moment, and began to leave. A few paces away he paused, turned, and said softly, with a catch in his voice, 'I shall always love you.'

A long way down the road, Carlo and the captain, both of them covered in fine beige dust, ruefully inspected their vehicle. It had no wheels and the interior was piled high with a smoking stack of manure.

That evening the captain noticed an exquisitely embroidered waistcoat hanging over the back of a chair in the kitchen. He picked it up and held it against the light; the velvet was richly scarlet, and the satin lining was sewn in with tiny conscientious threads that looked as though they could only have been done by the fingers of a diminutive sylph. In gold and yellow thread he saw languid flowers, soaring eagles, and leaping fish. He ran his finger over the embroidery and felt the density of the designs. He closed his eyes and realised that each figure recapitulated in relief the curves of the creature it portrayed.

Pelagia came in and caught him. She felt a rush of embarrassment, perhaps because she did not want him to know why she had made the article, perhaps because she had been rendered ashamed of its imperfections. He opened his eyes and held out the waistcoat to her. 'This is so beautiful,' he said, 'I have never seen anything as good as this that wasn't in a museum. Where does it come from?'

'I made it. And it's not so good.'

'Not so good?' he repeated disbelievingly. 'It's a masterpiece.'

Pelagia shook her head, 'It doesn't match up properly on both sides. They're supposed to be mirror images of each other, and if you look, this eagle is at a different angle to that one, and this flower is supposed to be the same size as that one, but it's bigger.'

The captain clicked his tongue disapprovingly, 'Symmetry is only a property of dead things. Did you ever see a tree or a mountain that was symmetrical? It's fine for buildings, but if you ever see a symmetrical human face, you will have the impression that you ought to think it beautiful, but that in fact you find it cold. The human heart likes a little disorder in its geometry, Kyria Pelagia. Look at your face in a mirror, Signorina, and you will see that one eyebrow is a little higher than the other, that the set of the lid of your left eye is such that the eye is a fraction more open than the other. It is these things that make you both attractive and beautiful, whereas . . . otherwise you would be a statue. Symmetry is for God, not for us.'

Pelagia pulled a sceptical expression, and prepared impatiently to dismiss his allegation that she was beautiful, but at that point she noticed that his nose was not perfectly straight. 'What is this?' asked the captain, pointing to an eagle, 'I mean, how is it done?'

Pelagia pointed with her finger, 'This is fil-tiré, and that is feston.' He was able to appreciate the articulateness of her forefinger and the smell of rosemary in her hair, but he shook his head, 'I'm none the wiser. Will you sell it to me? How much do you want for it?'

'It's not for sale,' she said.

'O please, Kyria Pelagia, I will pay you in anything you want. Drachmas, lire, tins of ham, bottled olives, tobacco. Name a price. I have some British gold sovereigns.'

Pelagia shook her head; there was little reason now why she should not sell it, but the captain had made her proud enough of it to induce her to want to keep it, and besides, selling it to him would have been, in some indefinable way, quite wrong.

'I am very sorry,' said the captain, 'but that reminds me; how much rent do you want?'

'Rent?' said Pelagia, almost dumbfounded.

'Did you think I intended to live here for nothing?' He reached into his pocket and produced a large chunk of salami, saying, 'I thought you might like to borrow this from the Officers' Mess. I have already given a slice to the "cat", and I think that now we are friends.'

'You've turned Psipsina and Lemoni into collaborators,' observed Pelagia wryly, 'and you'd better ask my father about the rent.'

A week later, after it had been reclaimed and given a new set of wheels, the engine of the jeep would explode spectacularly as it was being driven up the hairpin bends of the hill to Kastro. The driver was a very young lance-bombardier who had been a tenor in Corelli's opera society, and had been waiting for the war to end so that he could marry his childhood love in Palermo.

By that time Mandras was in the heart of Peloponnisos, widowmaking and rebuilding his dream of Pelagia.

A Discourse on Mandolins
and a Concert

The doctor awoke at his usual hour, and departed for the kapheneion without awaking Pelagia; he had looked at her, curled up in her blankets upon the kitchen floor, and had not had the heart to disturb her. It did offend his sense of the natural decency of arising promptly upon the hour, but on the other hand she worked hard for him, and had already become exhausted by the difficulties of coping with the war. Besides all that, she looked very fetching with her hair disarrayed upon the bolster, the blanket pulled over her nose, and only one small ear completely exposed. He had stood over her, appreciating the paternal emotions that arose in his breast, and then had not been able to prevent himself from leaning down and peering into the ear in order to check that it was in good condition; there was one very small flake of skin suspended upon the tip of a gossamer hair at the junction of the auricle and the external auditory meatus, but the overall impression was one of perfect health. The doctor smiled down upon her, and then made himself miserable by reflecting that one day she would grow old, bent, and wrinkled, the sweet beauty would desiccate and disappear like dry leaves so that no one would know that it had ever been there. Seized by an impression of the preciousness of the ephemeral, he knelt down and kissed her on the cheek. He went to the kapheneion in a tragic mood that sat oddly with the serenity of a cloudless morning.

The captain, awakened by a sharp twinge from a haemorrhoid, came out into the kitchen, saw Pelagia fast asleep, and did not know what to do. He would have liked to have brewed himself a cup of coffee and eaten a piece of fruit, but he too was captivated by the appealing tranquillity of the sleeping girl, and felt that it would have been a desecration to awake her by clattering about. In addition he did not want to cause her any embarrassment that might arise from being in his presence in night-clothes, and, besides, it was terrible to be reminded of the shame of having displaced a rightful owner from her own bed. He looked down upon her and experienced the urge to crawl in beside her – nothing could have seemed more natural – but instead he returned to his room and took Antonia out of her case. He began to practise fingerings with his left hand, sounding the notes minimally by hammering on and pulling off with his fingers rather than by using a plectrum. Tiring of this, he took a plectrum and laid the side of his right hand across the bridge so that he could mute the strings and play 'sordo'. It made a sound very like a violin playing pizzicato, and with great concentration he set himself to playing a very difficult and rapid piece by Paganini that consisted entirely of that effect.

Half way between sleep and waking, Pelagia's lucid dream rook on the distant rhythm of the piece. She was remembering the day before, when the captain had actually arrived at the house on a grey horse that he had borrowed from one of the soldiers who performed the curfew patrol each night. This capricious beast had been trained to

caracole, and his owner had taken to impressing
girls by making the beast execute this pretty trick
whenever he saw one. The horse had soon cottoned
onto the idea, and now readily did it unbidden
whenever he came across a human in skirts who
had long hair and bright eyes. All the soldiers were
very envious of this animal, and its rider was always
prepared to lend it to officers on the understanding
that advantageous adjustments would be made to
duty rosters. On the day that the captain borrowed
it, its rider would be excused from latrine fatigues.

When Corelli had arrived at the entrance of the
yard and Pelagia had looked up from brushing her
goat, the horse had pricked up its ears and caracoled. The captain had raised his cap, smiling
broadly, and Pelagia had felt a dart of pleasure
such as she had seldom experienced before. It was
the kind of pleasure that one feels when a dancer
who has been kicking his legs impossibly high
suddenly somersaults backwards, or when an apple
rolls off a shelf, strikes a spoon, and the spoon
spins up into the air and lands in a cup, scoop
downwards, and comes tinkling to a rest as though
it had been tossed there on purpose. Pelagia had

beheld Corelli and the exhibitionist horse, and she had smiled and clapped spontaneously whilst Corelli's face had split from ear to ear in an enormous grin like that of a little boy who has at last been given a football after years of whining and begging.

In her dream the horse caracoled to the tempo of Paganini, and its rider at one moment had the face of Mandras, and at another that of the captain. She found this annoying, and made a mental effort to reduce the faces to a single one. It became Mandras, but she found this unsatisfactory, and changed it to Corelli. Had there been anybody in the room, they would have seen her smiling in her sleep; she was reliving the jingle of brass, the creak of leather, the sharp sweet smell of horse's sweat, the intelligent pricking of its ears, the tiny sideways motion of the hooves as they struck the dust and stones of the road, the tensing and relaxing of the muscles in the haunches of the horse, the grand gesture of the smiling soldier as he swept off his cap.

Sitting on the bed, Corelli became so absorbed in his practising that he forgot the sleeping girl, and he began to work on getting his tremolo up to speed; it was deeply annoying to him that every day he would have to play for at least a quarter of an hour before he could make it steady and continuous, and he commenced the exercise by mechanically clicking the plectrum backwards and forwards at half speed across the top pair of trebles.

Pelagia awoke ten minutes later. Her eyes flicked open, and she lay there for a second, wondering if she was still asleep. There was a most beautiful noise coming from somewhere in the house, as though a thrush had adapted its song to human tastes and was pouring out its heart on a branch by the sill. A shaft of sunlight was breaking through the window, she felt too hot, and she realised that she had overslept. She sat up, wrapped her arms about her knees, and listened. Then she picked up her clothes from where they lay beside her pallet, and went to dress in her father's room, still attending to the trilling of the mandolin.

Corelli heard the metallic clatter of a spoon in a pan, realised that she had risen at last, and, still clutching the mandolin, came out into the kitchen. 'Sewage?' she asked, offering him a cup of the

48

bitter liquid that nowadays passed for coffee. He smiled and took it, realising that he was still very sore from riding that horse, and that he was still very relieved that he had not suddenly fallen off; it had been a near thing when it had started to dance like that. His thighs ached and it was painful to walk, so he sat down. 'That was very beautiful,' commented Pelagia.

The captain looked at his mandolin as though he was blaming it for something, 'I was only practising tremolando scales.'

'I don't care,' she replied, 'I still liked it, it made waking up very easy.'

He looked unhappy, 'I'm sorry I woke you up, I didn't mean to.'

'That's very beautiful,' she said, pointing at the instrument with a spoon, 'the decoration is wonderful. Does all that improve the sound?'

'I doubt it,' said the captain, turning it around in his hands. He himself had forgotten how exquisite it was. It was purfled about the rim of the soundbox with trapezia of shimmering mother-of-pearl, and it had a black strikeplate in the shape of a clematis flower, inlaid with multicoloured blossoms that were purely the result of an exuberant craftsman's imagination. The ebony diapason was marked at the fifth, seventh, and twelfth frets with a pattern of ivory dots, and the rounded belly of it was composed of tapering strips of close-grained maple, separated skilfully by thin fillets of rosewood. The machine heads were finished in the shape of ancient lyres, and, Pelagia noted, the strings themselves were decorated at the silver tailpiece with small balls of brightly coloured fluff. 'I suppose you don't want me to touch it,' she said, and he clutched it tightly to his chest.

'My mother dropped it once, and for a moment I thought I was going to kill her. And some people have greasy fingers.'

Pelagia was offended, 'I don't have greasy fingers.'

The captain noted her aggrieved expression, and explained, 'Everyone has greasy fingers. You have to wash and then dry your hands before you touch the strings.'

'I like the little balls of fluff,' said Pelagia.

Corelli laughed, 'They're stupid, I don't even know why they're there. It's traditional.'

She sat down opposite him on the bench and asked, 'Why do you play it?'

'What an odd question. Why does one do anything? Do you mean, what led me to start?'

She shrugged her shoulders, and he said, 'I used to play the violin. A lot of violinists play one of these because they're tuned the same, you see.' Contemplatively he ran a fingernail across the strings to illustrate his point, a point which Pelagia, for the sake of simplicity, pretended to see. 'You can play violin music on one of these, except that you have to put in tremolos where a violin would have one sustained note.' He executed a quick tremolo to illustrate this second point. 'But I gave up the violin because, however much I tried, it just came out sounding like cats. I'd look up and the yard would be full of them, all yowling. No, seriously, it was like a tribe of cats or even worse, and the neighbours kept complaining. One day my uncle gave me Antonia, which used to belong to his own uncle, and I discovered that with frets on the fingerboard I could be a good musician. So there you are.'

Pelagia smiled, 'So do cats like the mandolin?'

'This is a little known fact,' he said in a confidential manner, 'but cats like anything in the soprano range. They don't like things that are alto, so you can't play a guitar or a viola to a cat. They just walk out with their tails in the air. But they do like a mandolin.'

'So the cats and the neighbours were both happy with the change?'

He nodded happily, and continued, 'And another thing. People don't realise how many of the great masters wrote for the mandolin. Not just Vivaldi and Hummel, but even Beethoven.'

'Even Beethoven,' repeated Pelagia. It was one of those mysterious, awesome, mythical names that implied the ultimate possibilities of human achievement, a name that in fact meant nothing at all specific to her, since she had never knowingly heard a single piece of his music. She knew simply that it was the name of an almighty genius.

'When the war's over,' said Corelli, 'I am going to become a professional concert player, and one day I am going to write a proper concerto in three movements, for mandolin and small orchestra.'

'You're going to be rich and famous then?' she said teasingly.

'Poor but happy. I'd have to take another job as well. What do you dream about? Being a doctor, you said.'

Pelagia shrugged, distorting her lips into an expression of resignation and scepticism. 'I don't know,' she said at last. 'I know I want to do something, but I don't know what it is. They don't let women become doctors, do they?'

'You can have bambinos. Everyone should have bambinos. I'm going to have thirty or forty.'

'Your poor wife,' said Pelagia disapprovingly.

'I don't have one, so I might have to adopt.'

'You could be a teacher. That way you could be with children in the daytime and have time for music in the evening. Why don't you play me something?'

'O God, whenever people ask me to play something I forget what pieces I know. And I always depend on having the music in front of me. It's very bad. I know, I'll play you a polka. It's by Persichini.' He positioned the mandolin, and played two notes. He stopped, explaining, 'It slipped.

That's the trouble with these roundbacks from Naples. I often think I should get a Portuguese one with a flat back, but where does one get one of those in times of war?' He followed this rhetorical question with the same two notes, ritardando, played four quaver chords, then a bar which disrupted one's expectations by the introduction of a rest and a pair of semiquavers, and very shortly broke into cascades of chorded and unchorded semiquavers that left Pelagia open-mouthed. She had never before heard such elaborate virtuosity, and never before had she found a piece of music to be so full of surprises. There were sudden, flashing tremolos at the beginning of bars, and places where the music hesitated without losing its tempo, or sustained the same speed despite appearing to halve or double it. Best of all, there were places where a note so high in pitch that it could barely be sounded descended at exhilarating pace down through the scale, and fell upon a reverberant bass note that barely had had time to ring before there came a sweet alternation of bass and treble. It made her want to dance or do something foolish.

She watched wonderingly as the fingers of his left hand crawled like a powerful and menacing spider up and down the diapason. She saw the tendons moving and rippling beneath the skin, and then she saw that a symphony of expressions was passing over his face; at times serene, at times suddenly furious, occasionally smiling, from time to time stern and dictatorial, and then coaxing and gentle. Transfixed by this, she realised suddenly that there was something about music that had never been revealed to her before: it was not merely the production of sweet sound; it was, to those who understood it, an emotional and intellectual odyssey. She watched his face, and forgot to attend any more to the music; she wanted to share the journey. She leaned forward and clasped her hands together as though she were at prayer.

The captain repeated the first part, and concluded it suddenly on a spread chord that he muted immediately so that Pelagia felt deprived. 'There you are,' he said, wiping his forehead with his sleeve.

She felt excited, she wanted to jump up and perform a pirouette. Instead she said, 'I just don't understand why an artist like you would descend to being a soldier.'

He frowned, 'Don't have any silly ideas about soldiers. Soldiers have mothers, you know, and most of us end up as farmers and fishermen like everyone else.'

'I mean that for you it must be a waste of time, that's all.'

'Of course it's a waste of time.' He stood up and looked at his watch, 'Carlo should have been here by now. I'll just go and put Antonia away.' He looked at her with one eyebrow raised, 'By the way, Signorina, I couldn't help noticing that you have a derringer in the pocket of your apron.'

Pelagia's heart sank, and she began to tremble. But the captain continued, 'I understand why you should want to have it, and in fact I haven't seen it at all. But you must realise what would happen if someone else saw it. Especially a German. Just be more discreet.'

She looked up at him, appealing with her eyes, and he smiled, touched her shoulder, tapped the side of his nose with his forefinger, and winked.

After he had gone the thought occurred to

Pelagia that by now they could have poisoned the captain a hundred times over if they had ever wanted to. They could have extracted aconite from monkshood, they could have gathered hemlock, or stopped his heart with digitalis, and the authorities would never have known why he had died. She slipped her hand into the pocket of her apron and slid a finger round the trigger with that familiar motion that she had practised a hundred times. She weighed it in her hand. It was good of the captain to let her know that he respected her need for safety, for the reassurance and the defiance that proceeded from the ownership of a weapon. And you don't poison a musician, not even an Italian; it would have been as abominable as smearing excrement upon the tombstone of a priest.

That evening the doctor himself demanded a concert, and he and Pelagia found themselves outdoors in the yard whilst the captain spread a sheet of music upon the table, and both illuminated it and prevented it from being carried away by the breeze by placing a lantern on its upper edge. Solemnly he sat down and began to tap the striking plate with the plectrum.

The doctor raised his eyebrows in perplexity. This tapping seemed to go on for a very long time. Perhaps the captain was trying to establish a rhythm. Perhaps this was one of those minimalist pieces he had heard about, which was all squawks and squeaks and no melody, and perhaps this was the introduction. He looked at Pelagia, and she caught his glance and raised her hands in incomprehension. There was more tapping. The doctor peered at the captain's face, which was rapt in deep concentration. The doctor always found that in incomprehensible artistic situations like this his backside inevitably began to itch. He shifted his seat, and then lost patience, 'Excuse me, young man, but what on earth are you doing? This is not quite what my daughter led me to expect.'

'Damn,' exclaimed the captain, his concentration utterly destroyed, 'I was just about to start playing.'

'Well, about time too, I should think. What on earth were you doing? What is it? Some ghastly modern twaddle called "Two Tin Cans, a Carrot, and Dead Harlot?"'

Corelli was offended, and spoke with a distinct

tone of lofty disdain, 'I am playing one of Hummel's Concertos for Mandolin. The first forty-five and a half bars are for the orchestra, allegro moderato e grazioso. You have to imagine the orchestra. Now I've got to begin all over again.'

The doctor glared at him, 'I'm damned if I'm going to sit through all that tapping again, and I'm damned if I can imagine an orchestra. Just play your parts.'

The captain glared back, clearly indicating his conviction that the doctor was a complete philistine. 'If I do that,' he said, 'I'll start getting confused about when I'm supposed to come in, and that, in a concert hall, would be a disaster.'

The doctor stood up and waved his arm about to take in the olive tree, the goat, the house, the night sky above. 'Ladies and gentlemen,' he bawled, 'I apologise for disrupting the concert.' He turned to Corelli, 'Is this a concert hall? And do my eyes deceive me, or is there not one orchestra present? Do my eyes perceive a single trombone? The smallest and most insignificant violin? Where, pray, is the conductor, and where are the royalty draped in jewellery?'

The captain sighed in resignation, Pelagia looked at him sympathetically, and the doctor added, 'And another thing. Whilst you are tapping away and imagining your orchestra, you are exchanging one stupid expression for another. How are we supposed to concentrate in front of such a gallery?'

WH S LITTLE READS

£1

voucher

£1.00 OFF WHEN YOU BUY THE
FULL-LENGTH EDITION OF THIS BOOK*

**To the Customer: Present this voucher at participating
WHSmith stores and redeem it for £1.00 off the price of
the full-length edition of Captain Corelli's Mandolin*.**

Terms & Conditions: 1. This voucher entitles you to
£1.00 off the price of the full-length edition of
Captain Corelli's Mandolin*. 2. Offer valid in
participating WHSmith High Street and Travel stores,
subject to availability, while stocks last. 3. Voucher valid
from
19 April 2003 until 31 March 2004 inclusive.
4. Cannot be exchanged for any other merchandise.
5. Only one voucher per transaction. 6. Only original,
unaltered vouchers will be accepted. WHSmith reserves
the right to reject any voucher it deems, in its sole
discretion, to have been forged, defaced or otherwise
tampered with. 7. Cash redemption value 0.001p.
Promoter: WH Smith Retail Limited, Greenbridge Road,
Swindon, Wiltshire SN3 3RX.

**TO THE STORE: PLEASE SCAN VOUCHER AND PRODUCT.
DO NOT 'MINT RETURN'. DESTROY VOUCHER.**